In 2019, Weibo was the largest social media site in China. More than 5 million people used it every day.

Dr. Li Wenliang Warns Us about *a Virus*

1

Dr. Li Wenliang was an eye doctor in Wuhan, China. In December 2019, Wenliang noticed something strange. Some patients had a mysterious new virus. He tried to warn the people he worked with about it. They did not listen. Wenliang did not report what he saw to the Chinese government. For that reason, the authorities thought he was spreading rumors.

Wenliang was on social media. He used a Chinese app called Weibo. On February 1, 2020, he wrote an update. He said, "The dust has settled, and the diagnosis is finally confirmed." It was his last post. Dr. Wenliang had caught the new virus. People soon realized that his warning was true. The virus he had caught was COVID-19. He died from it. He was only 34 years old.

People wanted to honor Wenliang after his death. They found his comment on Weibo. They wrote comments on his post. It was their way of saying "thank you" for trying to help.

People shared comments about Wenliang on Weibo, a social media app.

SPREADING THE WORD People started to think of Wenliang as a hero. In China, they were upset with the government. They wished Wenliang's words had been shared sooner. They wanted to know why they were not told important information. The Chinese government started giving people daily updates about the virus. It told people how many cases of the virus it knew about. More people were able to be tested for COVID-19.

Memorials for Wenliang exist around the world.

1 million Number of comments Wenliang received on his social media.

Wenliang warned people about COVID-19. • Wenliang died from COVID-19. • The Chinese government started being more truthful with its people because of Wenliang.

Dr. Zhang Jixian Treats First *COVID Patients*

2

Dr. Zhang Jixian is thought to be the first doctor to treat COVID-19 patients. Jixian worked with viruses before. She worked in a hospital during an **outbreak** of SARS in 2003. SARS is a contagious illness caused by a coronavirus. That work helped her know what to look out for. She knew the signs of an **epidemic**.

Jixian worked at a hospital in Wuhan, China. She had two patients come see her in December 2019. They had symptoms that confused her. She looked at the insides and outsides of their bodies. She also took samples of their blood. Jixian found that what they had was new and different. It could also spread easily between people. She told the Center for Disease Control in Wuhan about it. They organized some testing. Jixian had to handle other things on her own.

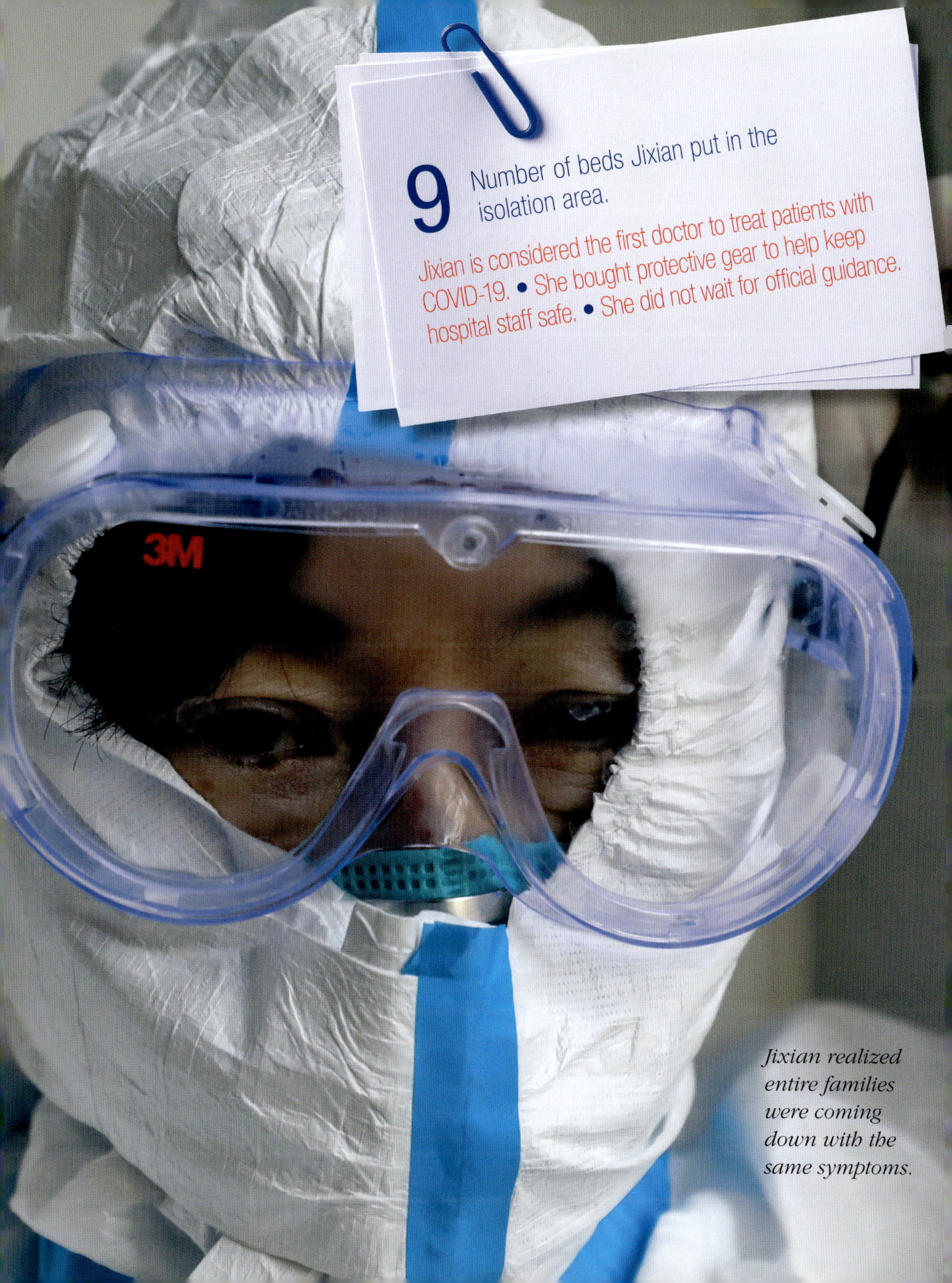

9 Number of beds Jixian put in the isolation area.

Jixian is considered the first doctor to treat patients with COVID-19. • She bought protective gear to help keep hospital staff safe. • She did not wait for official guidance.

Jixian realized entire families were coming down with the same symptoms.

Jixian wanted to make sure patients and staff at the hospital were safe. She quickly made an area just for the patients with the virus. She set up China's first **isolation** room. The patients were kept away from other people. Jixian bought special canvas. People wore it under their work clothes. It could protect them from the virus. She made sure doctors and nurses wore other safety equipment too.

Think About It Why do you think Jixian rushed to make an isolation room? Should she have waited for the CDC to help her through the whole process?

Personal protective equipment (PPE) was especially hard to find at the beginning of the pandemic.

Jacinda Ardern Goes on *Early Lockdown*

3

Jacinda Ardern was the prime minister of New Zealand. She took office in 2017. She was 37 years old. The COVID-19 virus hit the country in March 2020. Ardern did not take it lightly. She worked with the New Zealand government. They came up with a plan.

The virus had spread in other countries. Leaders were trying to keep the virus from spreading further. People tried social distancing. They wore masks. There were reminders to keep their hands clean. However, this did not seem to do much to stop the spread.

On March 23, 2020, New Zealand's leaders made a promise. They would find a way to **eliminate** the virus in the country. New Zealand only had about 100 cases. Ardern wanted to act quickly to stop it from getting worse. She said it was best to "go hard, go early." She

LOCKDOWN LEVELS New Zealand had different levels of lockdowns. The highest level was severe. The whole country was on the highest level of lockdown from March 25 to April 27 in 2020. By June in 2020, they were on the lowest level. This meant that businesses could be open. Kids went back to school. Public places could be used. People still needed to socially distance. They still wore masks in public places.

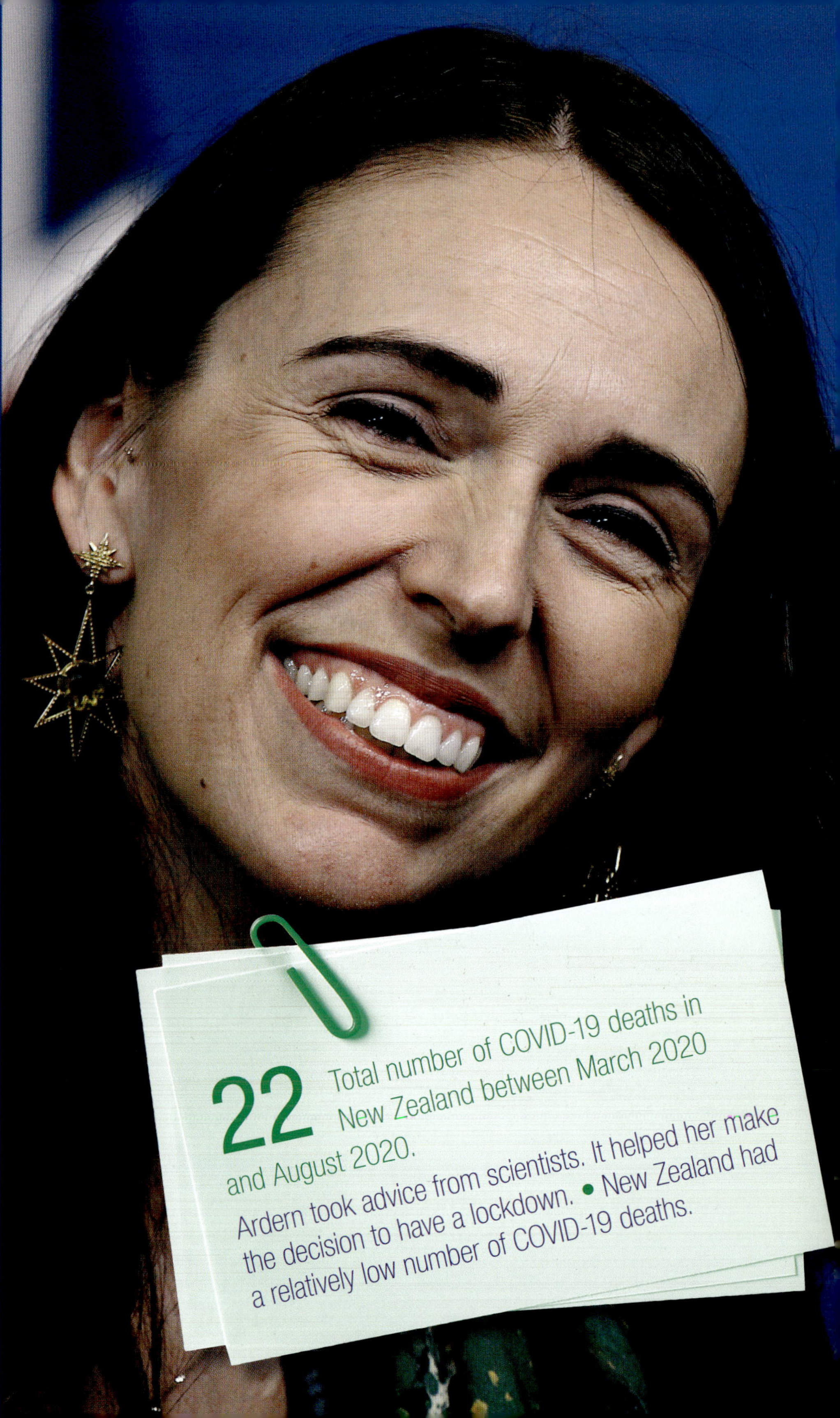

22 Total number of COVID-19 deaths in New Zealand between March 2020 and August 2020.

Ardern took advice from scientists. It helped her make the decision to have a lockdown. • New Zealand had a relatively low number of COVID-19 deaths.

worked with scientists to come up with a plan. She put the country on **lockdown**. People could not come to visit. Only businesses like grocery stores and hospitals could stay open.

By August 2020, the country had gone 100 days without any new COVID-19 cases. People asked Ardern how New Zealand did it. She said it was because of the "go hard, go early" plan.

Think About It

What if you were prime minister of New Zealand? What would you have done differently?

Some people did not like Jacinda's plan. They protested.

Leo Varadkar Helps by Becoming *a Doctor... Again*

4

Leo Varadkar served as the prime minister of Ireland from 2017 until 2020 and again starting in 2022. But he was not always in politics. He had gone to medical school. He was a doctor in Ireland before he became prime minister.

Some people in Ireland were not big fans of Varadkar. They thought he was not true to his word. But things changed when COVID-19 reached the country. Varadkar canceled St. Patrick's Day celebrations. He closed schools and some businesses. Varadkar also made sure there were ways to test for the virus.

Varadkar was inspired by his family. Varadkar's husband, his two sisters, and their husbands were all health care workers. He saw that they were working hard during the **pandemic**. He was proud of them.

70,000 Number of people who were called back to the medical field after Varadkar.

Varadkar worked as a doctor before he was prime minister. • His family members work in health care. • He registered again as a medical doctor to help people with the virus.

Ireland did not have a St. Patrick's Day parade for two years. They finally had one in 2022.

Think About It Ireland's St. Patrick's Day parade was canceled two years in a row because of COVID-19. The parade is a popular event. Half a million people attend every year. What other crises might cancel such an important event? Think of crises from the past and present.

"Not all heroes wear capes. Some wear scrubs and gowns," he said.

Varadkar wanted to use his knowledge to help too. He told the country that he would work one day a week as a doctor. He took calls from people who thought they might have the virus. Varadkar did his work as prime minister at the same time.

Ireland still needed more help. The health ministry called anyone who used to work in the medical field to duty. Varadkar spoke to the people too. He asked the past medical workers to help if they could. Varadkar's words were a success. Health care workers came back to the hospitals.

Health care workers took many risks during the COVID-19 pandemic.

5

Dr. Anthony Fauci Brings Experience *to a Task Force*

Dr. Anthony Fauci works in the United States. He was the director of the National Institute of Allergy and **Infectious** Diseases (NIAID). Fauci had this role since 1984. He worked on HIV and AIDS research. He also worked with other virus epidemics. It was his job to find ways to stop diseases. He also tried to find ways to cure them.

In January 2020, President Donald Trump created a special group. It was called the White House Coronavirus Task Force. The group was made up of experts. They study viruses. They know a lot about other medical issues too. Fauci's job was to research the virus. He told others what he thought could help keep the virus from spreading.

Fauci became well-known when the outbreak of the virus hit the United States. He gave interviews and went on TV. He told people that they needed to wash their hands and wear face masks. He asked them to socially distance. He also said to stay home whenever possible.

Fauci was on TV a lot when COVID-19 first started. He spoke at press conferences. News reporters asked him questions. He gave interviews. People began to recognize him. He became the face of all the scientists working to figure out the new virus. In 2022, Fauci stepped down as the director of NIAID.

1,400 Number of scientific works that Dr. Fauci has helped write. This includes textbooks.

Fauci worked on research for HIV and AIDS. • Fauci was a member of a task force. Its role is to help learn about and fight COVID-19. • He was the face of the virus' task force.

Dr. Fauci worked for seven US presidents.

VIRUSES AND DISEASES Dr. Fauci worked in the medical field for a long time. He worked on research for many viruses and diseases. He researched HIV and AIDS. In 2003, a President's Emergency Plan for AIDS Relief was made. Fauci was one of the main doctors involved. He has also looked at diseases like Ebola and Zika.

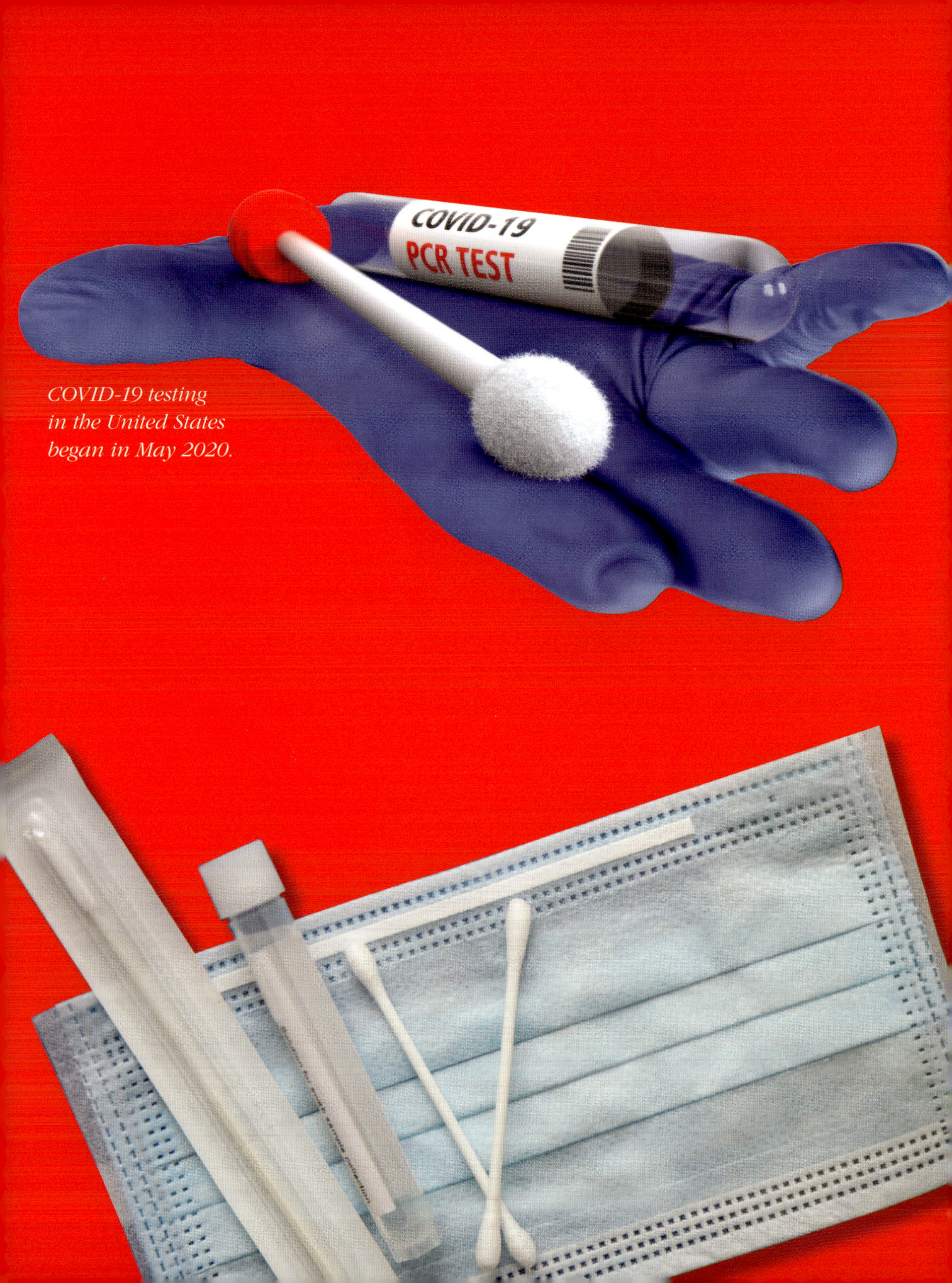

COVID-19 testing in the United States began in May 2020.

Emma Spiro & Kate Starbird Learn about the *Spread of Misinformation*

6

Emma Spiro is a sociologist. She studies human behavior. Kate Starbird is a researcher. They were coworkers at the University of Washington in Seattle. They started a big project together. In December 2019, they founded the Center for an Informed Public. They hoped that it would help people get important information.

A few months later, COVID-19 reached the United States. Scientists shared what they knew. Other scientists did not always agree. The public weighed in on the issues too. There was a lot of **misinformation**. Spiro and Starbird saw this as an opportunity. They could use their knowledge. They studied how information about COVID-19 spread.

Spiro and Starbird started doing research. They kept track of news reports. They also looked at data from social media. The two wrote an article in June 2020. They explained that false information is easy to spread. The internet makes it even easier.

Spiro and Starbird gave interviews. They explained how false information can affect people. They said that tech companies need to play a bigger role. The companies should make sure correct information is being shared.

2012 Year Dr. Spiro chose a subject to study. She focused her research on understanding how misinformation affects behavior during times of crisis.

Spiro and Starbird worked together to understand how misinformation spread. • They looked at how information spread on the news and on social media.

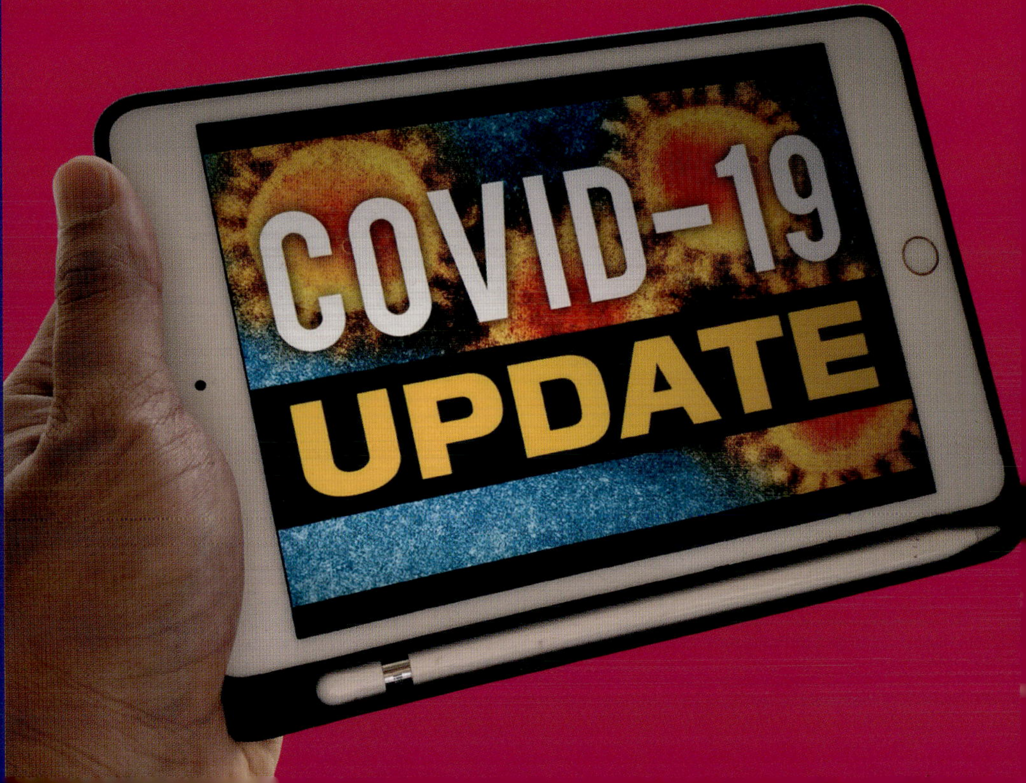

WHY MISINFORMATION HAPPENS During a crisis, there is always a lot of unknown information. Why did it happen? Who did it? What can we do to help? People try to make sense of things they do not understand during those times. Spiro and Starbird write about this in their article. They explain that some people will try to find things that make them feel better. They may find comfort in the misinformation and not want to seek out different points of view.

Misinformation is false or inaccurate information.

Think About It Can you think of any examples of misinformation in your own life? How was that information spread? How did it make you feel?

CNN politics

Fauci warns Congress that new US coronavirus cases could rise to 100,000 a day

By Clare Foran and Jamie Ehrlich, CNN

Updated 1902 GMT (0302 HKT) June 30, 2020

Using trusted news sources can help stop misinformation.

Lady Gaga Puts Together *a Benefit Concert*

7 Lady Gaga is a singer and an actress. She had an album coming out in April 2020. But she did not feel right releasing it. The COVID-19 pandemic had started. She knew there were important things happening in the world. She wanted to do something to help. So, she started working with a group called Global Citizen. The group helps people in **poverty**.

Lady Gaga started to plan a concert. It would be called One World: Together at Home. The concert would not happen in person. Instead, it would be **virtual**. The singer talked to 68 companies. She asked them to pay for it.

The concert would be free. However, there would be a way to donate money. The donations would go toward the World Health Organization. The concert could be

Lady Gaga speaks to viewers at home during her benefit concert.

$127 million Amount of money One World: Together at Home raised for COVID-19 relief.

Lady Gaga worked with Global Citizen to put together a virtual concert. • She raised over $35 million before the concert. • The money bought protective equipment for health care workers.

an effective way to raise money. It could also bring people some joy through music.

Lady Gaga also talked to other famous singers and performers. They gave time and money. Before the concert even happened, Lady Gaga was able to raise $35 million. It was all donated to COVID-19 relief. The concert itself was a success. Around 270 million people watched worldwide.

HOW THE DONATIONS HELPED The donated money was given out over a year. It helped bring emergency aid to over 162 countries. It helped buy protective gear for health care workers. Some people would have struggled without the help.

Andrew Brooks Develops *a New Test*

8

Andrew Brooks was a research professor. He studied microbiology and immunology. He worked at Rutgers University. The college is in New Jersey.

In April 2020, there were not many ways to get tested for COVID-19. There were long lines. People had to wait for hours. The tests that people took were nose or throat swabs. Those swabs could be uncomfortable. Brooks had a way to make more tests available. He also figured out how to make them easier for people to take.

Brooks had learned a lot while working in labs. He had done **genetic testing** with saliva. He knew the science behind it. Brooks thought he could make a saliva COVID-19 test that was easy to administer. So, he worked with two companies. They were successful. Brooks made the first saliva test for COVID-19.

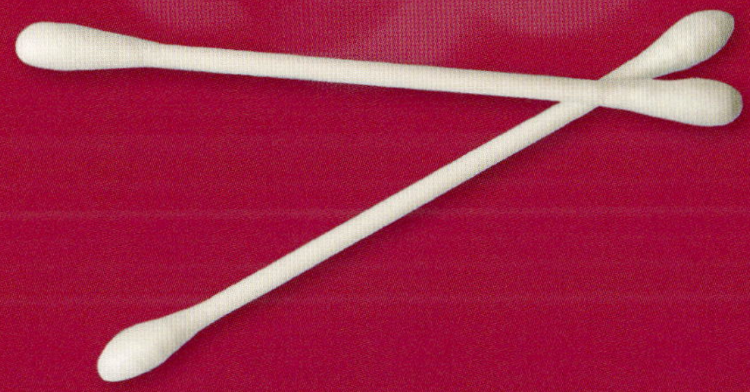

The Food and Drug Administration (FDA) gave the test its approval. This meant the FDA thought the test was safe and worked well. However, the test Brooks had made was only a sample. He did not have enough resources to make enough tests for the whole country.

The White House learned about the work Brooks was doing. It gave Brooks the money he needed to make many tests. People could now take a COVID-19 test without having to swab their nose or throat. The saliva test made testing more accessible. Now, people could know right away when they had the virus. More than four million tests were taken in less than a year.

4 million Number of people who used the saliva test in the first year.

Brooks developed a saliva COVID-19 test. • Brooks's test helped make sure many more people could get tested for COVID-19.

Beginning in 2022, millions of free at-home COVID tests were sent to people across the United States.

Katalin Karikó Creates a New *Vaccine Technology*

9

Katalin Karikó grew up in Hungary. She went to college to become a scientist. In 1985, she moved to the United States. A few years later, she got a job at the University of Pennsylvania. Karikó spent a lot of her time in science labs.

Karikó worked with another scientist. They were studying mRNA. That stands for messenger RNA. It gives the body information. It can help the body fight off disease. It can also be used for medicines and vaccines. Karikó and her coworker wanted to make better vaccines with it. Vaccines used to be made with a very small amount of a virus. However, Karikó and her partner thought they could make a new type. It would not need the existing virus. Instead, it could use mRNA to make proteins. The proteins could help the body fight off sickness.

Studying mRNA could help scientists cure other diseases too.

Karikó needed more money to research mRNA. Yet, she was never given any **grants** to help her work. They were going to other types of research. Karikó thought what she was doing was important. She and her coworker kept working. They studied mRNA for more than 30 years.

When the COVID-19 pandemic hit, there was a big need for a new vaccine. The faster it could be made, the more people it could help. Scientists looked at Karikó's work. They decided to use mRNA for a COVID-19 vaccine.

The Moderna COVID-19 vaccine was known as mRNA-1273.

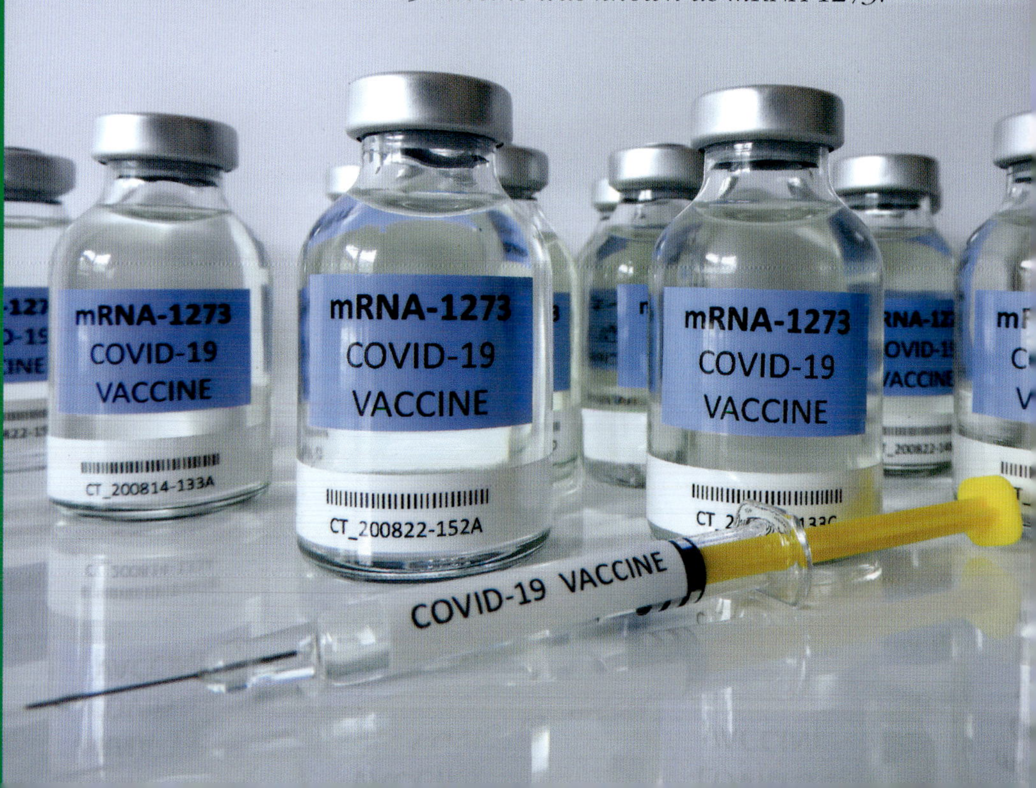

WHAT'S THE DIFFERENCE? Karikó worked on mRNA for her entire career. However, the COVID-19 vaccine is the first to use it. Traditional vaccines use a small, weakened amount of a virus. The virus is inactive. It is injected into the person. The body's immune system starts to fight the virus. It learns how to work against it. If the person later catches the virus, the body can fight it off. However, mRNA vaccines work differently. A small amount of a protein is added to some lipids, or fats. Then it is injected as a vaccine. The protein itself works with the body's immune system.

It can take many years for a vaccine to be approved. But the COVID-19 vaccine was approved in less than a year.

35 Number of years Karikó worked with mRNA during her career, as of 2024.

Karikó grew up in Hungary. • In the United States, she researched mRNA. • Her research was used to make COVID-19 vaccines.

Dolly Parton Donates *Money*

10

Dolly Parton is a singer and an actress. She is also a **philanthropist**. Parton spends a lot of her time and money helping other people. Students have received scholarships from Parton. She sends free books to children. She also donates money to hospitals and charities. When COVID-19 was officially called a pandemic, Parton decided to help. She told an interviewer, "I felt like this was the time for me to open my heart and my hand and try to help."

Parton is friends with a doctor at Vanderbilt University. The college is in Nashville, Tennessee. Parton visited him. They talked about the virus. She wanted to help. Parton decided to donate money to Vanderbilt. Vanderbilt University worked with a medical company called Moderna. It was researching how to make a

$1 million Amount of money Dolly Parton donated to COVID-19 research.

Parton's donation helped fund early stages of the COVID-19 vaccine. • She was listed as someone who helped make vaccine research possible. • She waited until other people had their vaccine before she got hers.

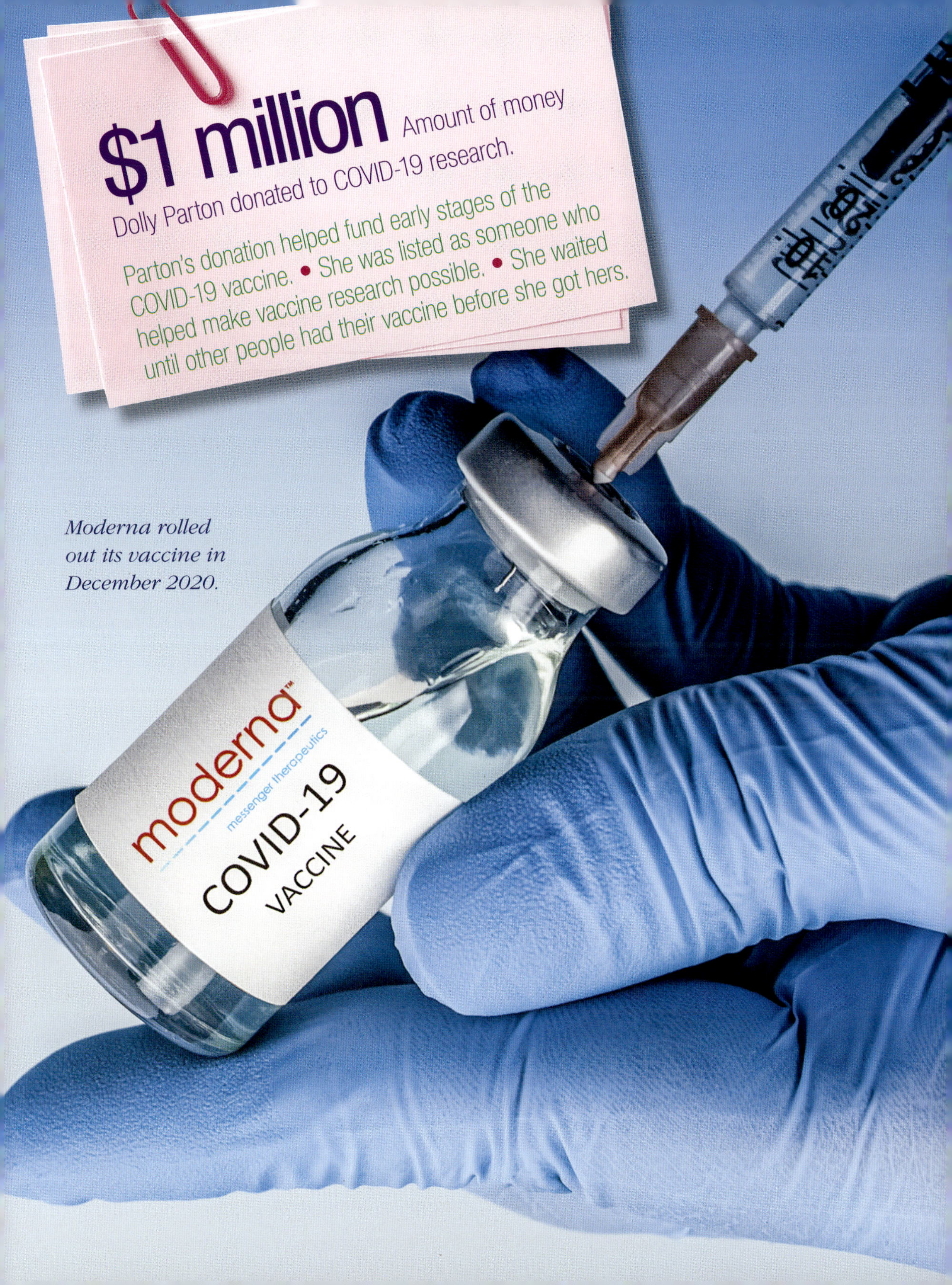

Moderna rolled out its vaccine in December 2020.

COVID-19 vaccine. Parton's money helped. It funded more research and equipment. It helped a vaccine get made. Parton put herself on a waiting list to get the vaccine.

Parton's charity Imagination Library sends free books to children under age 5.

WHY WAIT? Some people were surprised that Parton waited for a vaccine. They thought she would be one of the first people to get it. But Parton thought there were other people who needed it more. She did not want it to seem like she paid for a place in line.

Dr. Kizzmekia Corbett Leads the *Vaccine Team*

11

Dr. Kizzmekia Corbett is a scientist. She studies the way the human immune system reacts to viruses. She works with the National Institute of Health in the United States. Corbett works at the vaccine research center there. It is her job to help develop vaccines for different viruses.

Corbett works with mRNA. This molecule is a key part of the COVID-19 vaccine. Corbett was part of a team put together by Dr. Anthony Fauci. They worked on making the Moderna COVID-19 vaccine in 2020. Corbett was an important member.

Early in the pandemic, scientists were hopeful. They said that it might be possible for a vaccine to be made within a year. Corbett said she knew it could be done. She and the rest of the team worked hard. First, though, she

mRNA contains instructions that tell your body how to make proteins.

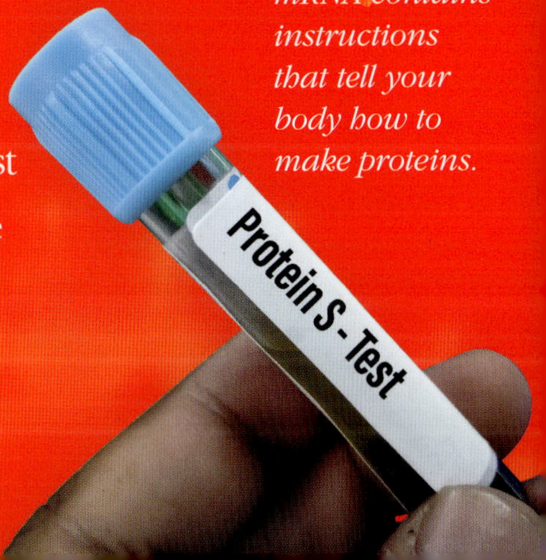

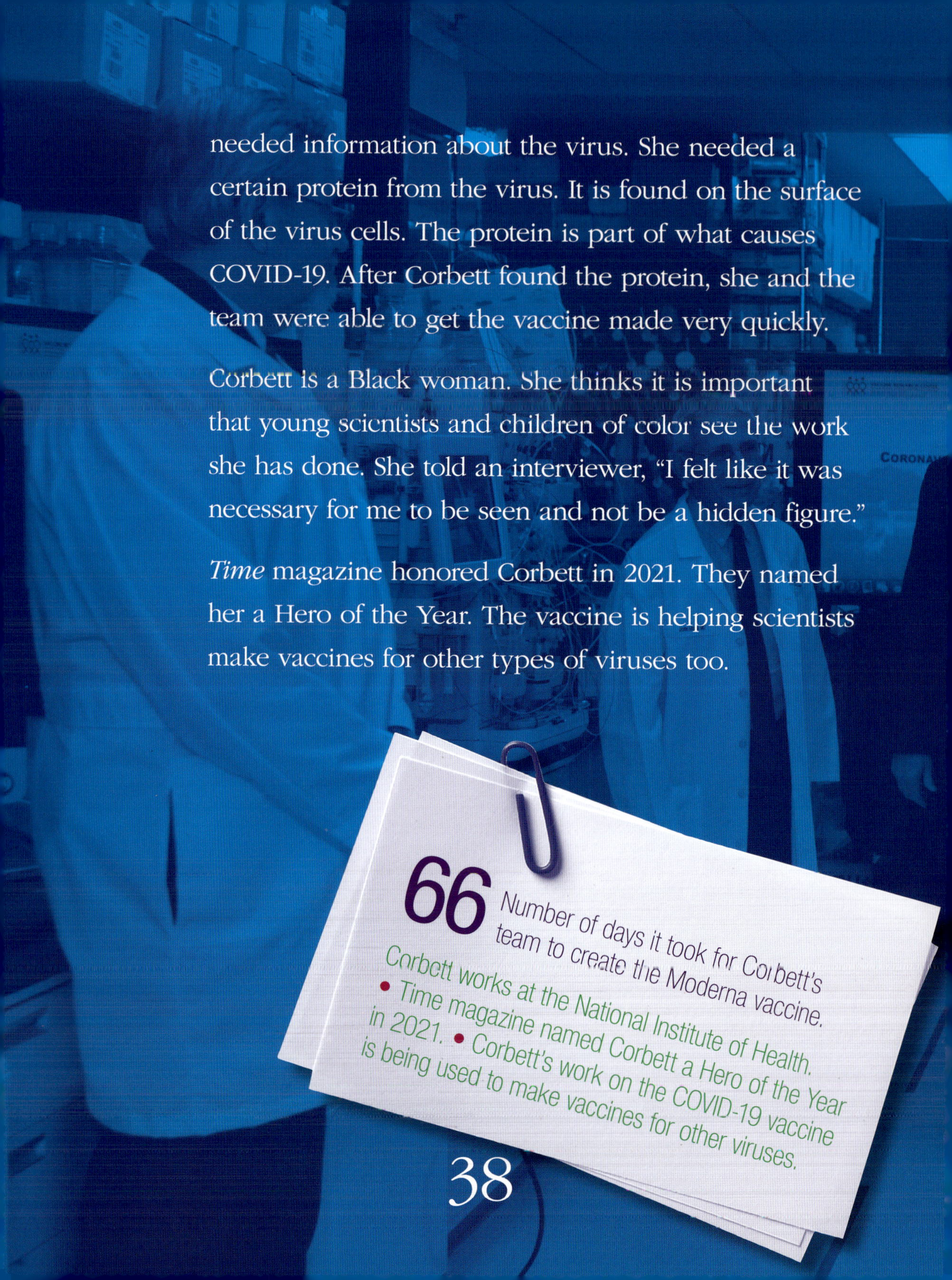

needed information about the virus. She needed a certain protein from the virus. It is found on the surface of the virus cells. The protein is part of what causes COVID-19. After Corbett found the protein, she and the team were able to get the vaccine made very quickly.

Corbett is a Black woman. She thinks it is important that young scientists and children of color see the work she has done. She told an interviewer, "I felt like it was necessary for me to be seen and not be a hidden figure."

Time magazine honored Corbett in 2021. They named her a Hero of the Year. The vaccine is helping scientists make vaccines for other types of viruses too.

66 Number of days it took for Corbett's team to create the Moderna vaccine.

Corbett works at the National Institute of Health. • Time magazine named Corbett a Hero of the Year in 2021. • Corbett's work on the COVID-19 vaccine is being used to make vaccines for other viruses.

In 2020, Corbett gave a tour of the vaccine lab to President Donald Trump and Dr. Fauci.

John Krasinski Brings Joy *to People*

12 John Krasinski is an actor and a director. He has starred in movies and TV shows. He was on a TV show called *The Office*. He is best known for being a comedy actor. He likes to make people laugh.

The United States went into lockdown in March 2020. This was difficult for people of all ages. They could not go to work or school. They could not see their families or friends. The news told a lot of sad stories. People were getting sick. Events were getting canceled. Krasinski saw that it was a hard time for a lot of people. He had an idea to help.

Krasinski posted on Twitter (now called X). He asked his followers to use the hashtag #SomeGoodNews. He wanted to hear happy stories. Thousands of people responded. Krasinski decided to make a show about it.

Krasinski used social media to find inspirational stories.

Krasinski made a small studio in his home. His kids drew a sign for him. He put together videos of the stories he had heard. He called the show *Some Good News*. He posted the show on YouTube. People could watch it for free. The show only told stories that would make people feel good.

Special guests would come on the show. In-person events had been canceled because of COVID-19. So, actors and musicians surprised fans virtually. A lot of high school students' proms were canceled. Krasinski made a special episode for them. He hosted a virtual prom. Famous singers gave them music to dance to.

The show only had eight episodes. In two months, though, it had more than 72 million views. People thought it was helpful seeing good news. It made them feel less alone. It made them happy during a sad and hard time.

Did You Know? Krasinski first had the idea for *Some Good News* back in 2013. He wanted a news show that was only happy stories.

8 Number of episodes of *Some Good News.*

Krasinski wanted to bring good news to people during COVID-19 lockdowns. • He started a YouTube series called *Some Good News.* • It got more than 72 million views.

People enjoyed watching Some Good News *on all electronic devices.*

How You Can Make a Change

Stay Healthy

A big part of helping in a pandemic is to stay healthy. Eating a diet of fresh food helps. Look for fruits and vegetables that are high in Vitamin C. Getting exercise and playing outdoors is good for the body too. The Centers for Disease Control and Prevention (CDC) has recommendations as well. The CDC recommends washing your hands often. If you need to sneeze or cough, make sure to cover your mouth. However, try not to cover it with your hands! If you do, be sure to wash your hands.

Donate

Ask a parent or a caregiver to help you give books away. You can donate them to a children's charity. Ask an adult to volunteer with you at a soup kitchen. Work with classmates to organize a fundraiser for your favorite charity.

Send Positive Messages

Health care workers work very hard. The pandemic has made them work even harder. One way to make a difference is to write special notes to them. You can draw or paint them special pictures and cards. You can write thank-you notes for all their work. This can help them feel appreciated.

Glossary

accessible
Easy to get.

eliminate
To get rid of.

epidemic
Widespread disease in a certain area during a certain time.

genetic testing
A way of testing that looks for changes in human DNA.

grant
Money given by a government or an organization.

immune system
A system in our bodies made up of organs, cells, and proteins that work together to protect from diseases, viruses, and other invaders.

infectious
Likely to spread an infection.

isolation
The state of being alone or or staying away from people.

lockdown
A security measure taken during emergencies that stops people from leaving or entering other buildings.

misinformation
Incorrect or misleading information.

outbreak
Sudden start of something that is unwelcome (usually war or disease).

pandemic
Disease that has spread worldwide or in an entire country.

philanthropist
A person who wants to help others and donates money to good causes.

poverty
Extremely poor.

virtual
Happening online.

For More Information

Books

London, Martha. *Vaccines.* Minneapolis: Bearport Publishing Company, 2023.

Sommer, Nathan. *The Coronavirus Pandemic.* Minneapolis: Bellwether Media, 2022.

Hanel, Rachael. *The COVID Pandemic.* Mankato, MN: Creative Education/Creative Paperbacks, 2023.

Websites

Global Citizen: One World Together at Home
www.globalcitizen.org/en/media/togetherathome/

National Geographic Kids: Facts About Coronavirus
https://kids.nationalgeographic.com/science/article/facts-about-coronavirus

YouTube: *Some Good News*
www.youtube.com/channel/UCOe_y6KKvS3PdIfb9q9pGug

 • Top Rank is an imprint of Black Rabbit Books. • Edited by Book Buddy Media • Designed by Danny Nanos • Photographs © Alamy: Alex Edelman, 17, 19, Penelope Barritt, 7, UPI, 38–39; AP: Newsroom FeatureChina, 2–3, 8–9; Dreamstime: Marco Iacobucci, 25, 44, Basphoto, 28–29, Kathyimages1, 17, Peter Kovác, 4; Shutterstock: Aitormmfoto, 15, Alexandros Michailidis, 11, 12, 14, Andrii Medvediuk, cover, 33, Andy Dean Photography, 16, Babul Hosen, 37, beton studio, 29, Billion Photos, 37, Cenz07, 36, Elzbieta Krzysztof, 32, Featureflash Photo Agency, 43, 45, Giovanni Cancemi, 20, Ink Drop, 20, 27, inProgressImaging, 13, J.J. Gouin, 5, Jag_cz, 43, 45, Kathy Hutchins, 34, Kravtzov, 18, 44, Mega Pixel, 21, metamorworks, 30–31, Olga Ganovicheva, 23, peenat, 10, Rahman Aziz, 22, Rose Carson, 42, s_bukley, 41, Seda Yalova, 35, Sergei Elagin, 6, solomon7, 40, StanislavSukhin, 2–3, Stock-Asso, 40, Sunny studio, 36, viewsphotos, 27, Yalcin Sonat, 24, 26, zimmytws, 23 • Printed in China.

Library of Congress Cataloging-in-Publication Data is available under LCCN 2023052904. • ISBN 9781645822912 (library binding), ISBN 9781645823230 (paperback), ISBN 9781645823551 (ebook)

Index

About the Author

Stephanie Loureiro is a writer and an editor who was born and raised in Southern California. When she is not working, she is lifting weights, singing loudly to Taylor Swift, or reading a good book. She currently lives in Idaho with her husband, daughter, and two lovable dogs.